KT-562-255

3|s WYE

WYE

2 9 SEP 2016

2 7 JUN 2019

1 5 NOV 2016

2 3 MAY 2015

1 3 APR 2017   2 2 OCT 2019

- 2 JUL 2015

2 3 JUL 2015

- 3 JUN 2017

- 8 JUL 2017

- 4 SEP 2015

- 7 OCT 2017

2 6 MAR 2016

1 3 MAR 2018

1 0 MAY 2016

- 5 JUL 2018   1 8 JAN 2020

WITHDRAWN

1 4 JUL 2016   2 4 MAY 2019

2 9 SEP 2022

- 8 SEP 2016

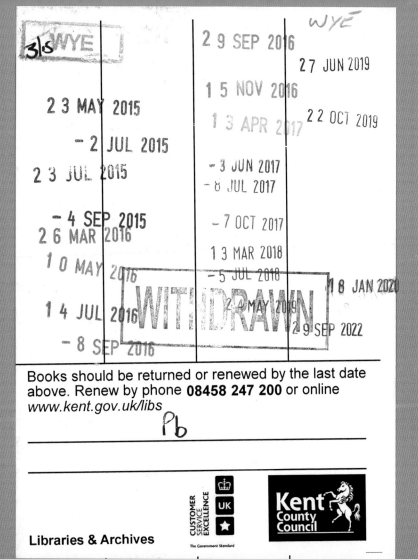

Books should be returned or renewed by the last date
above. Renew by phone **08458 247 200** or online
www.kent.gov.uk/libs

Pb

CUSTOMER
SERVICE
EXCELLENCE

UK

The Government Standard

Kent
County
Council

Libraries & Archives

WITHDRAWN

C333710009

For Joshua,
who first asked the question – F.S.

For Ruth, Johnny and Anna.
With all my love – B.C.

First published in Great Britain in 2013
by Orion Children's Books
a division of the Orion Publishing Group Ltd
Orion House
5 Upper St Martin's Lane
London WC2H 9EA
An Hachette UK Company

3 5 7 9 10 8 6 4

Text copyright © Francesca Simon 2013
Illustrations copyright © Ben Cort 2013

The rights of Francesca Simon and Ben Cort to be identified as
the author and illustrator of this work respectively have been asserted.

All rights reserved.
No part of this publication may be reproduced, stored in a retrieval system,
or transmitted, in any form or by any means, electronic, mechanical, photocopying,
recording or otherwise, without the prior permission of Orion Children's Books.

The Orion Publishing Group's policy is to use papers that are natural, renewable
and recyclable products and made from wood grown in sustainable forests.
The logging and manufacturing processes are expected to conform to
the environmental regulations of the country of origin.

A catalogue record for this book is available from the British Library.

ISBN 978 1 4440 0155 6

Printed and bound in Germany

www.orionbooks.co.uk

DO YOU SPEAK ENGLISH, MOON?

FRANCESCA SIMON
AND BEN CORT

Orion
Children's Books

"Do you speak English, Moon?

You do? That's great. Then we can talk.
I get lonely up here sometimes.
What I want to know is. . .

Do you go to the park, Moon?
I can go down the twisty turny slide.

Do you like chocolate ice cream?
That is my very best food.

Do you pretend you're a crocodile?
Do you play pirates?

So do I!
What else do you do?

Ahhh. I like watching too.

Can you see everything, Moon?

Can you see the city?

Can you see the sea?
Can you see under the sea?

Can you see the highest, highest mountain?

Can you see
the whole wide world?
Oh show me, show me!

Do you have lots of friends, Moon?
A billion, trillion, gazillion?

But they're all so far away.

Can you tell me some of their names?

Leo.
That's a nice name.

Milky Way. I like that one too.

But sometimes it's hard to get to sleep.
Do you get lonely up there, Moon?
Don't be lonely.

I'm here.
Anytime you want to talk.

Goodnight, Moon.
Goodnight."